A Minty Mess

READ ALL THE CANDY FAIRIES BOOKS!

Chocolate Dreams

Rainbow Swirl

Caramel Moon

Cool Mint

Magic Hearts

Gooey Goblins

The Sugar Ball

A Valentine's Surprise

Bubble Gum Rescue

Double Dip

Jelly Bean Jumble

The Chocolate Rose

A Royal Wedding

Marshmallow Mystery

Frozen Treats

The Sugar Cup

Sweet Secrets

Taffy Trouble

The Coconut Clue

Rock Candy Treasure

COMING SOON:

Peppermint Princess

Candy Fairies

A Minty Mess

HELEN
PERELMAN

ILLUSTRATED BY
ERICA-JANE WATERS

ALADDIN
NEW YORK LONDON TORONTO SYDNEY NEW DELHI

An imprint of Simon & Schuster Children's Publishing Division
1230 Avenue of the Americas, New York, New York 10020
First Aladdin paperback edition June 2016

Also available in an Aladdin hardcover edition.

Book designed by Karina Granda
The text of this book was set in Baskerville Book.
Manufactured in the United States of America 0516 OFF
2 4 6 8 10 9 7 5 3 1
Library of Congress Control Number 2016933488
ISBN 978-1-4814-4681-5 (hc)
ISBN 978-1-4814-4680-8 (pbk)
ISBN 978-1-4814-4682-2 (eBook)

To Caroline Jones Hubbell

LOLLIPOP LANDING
CANDY CASTLE
FRUIT CHEW MEADOW
RED LICORICE LAKE
PEPPERMINT GROVE
CHOCOLATE
GUMMY FOREST
BLACK LICORICE SWAMP

CHOCOLATE WOODS
CHOCOLATE FALLS
CARAMEL HILLS
CANDY CORN FIELDS
SOUR ORCHARD
RIVER
THE FROSTED MOUNTAINS
MARSHMALLOW MARSH
CANDY Kingdom
SUGAR VALLEY

Contents

CHAPTER 1

Sour Rain

Dash the Mint Fairy poked her head out her window. The rain was coming down hard in Peppermint Grove. All the candy mint plants and trees were pushed low to the ground from the heavy rain. "This is a minty mess," Dash grumbled.

She pulled the window closed and leaned

back in her chair. There had been rainy times before in Sugar Valley, but this was the longest stretch of rain she could remember. It had been raining for weeks. She looked out the window again and saw a sugar fly. She let the little messenger in and read the note.

Berry the Fruit Fairy had written that she would fly by soon with a surprise. Dash smiled. She wasn't sure how Berry was getting to Peppermint Grove. During this rainy time all the Candy Fairies had to be very careful. If a fairy's wings got wet, she couldn't fly. Leave it to her clever friend Berry to come up with a great idea.

Her friends had not gathered for Sun Dip for three days. Dash missed seeing her friends. She couldn't wait for Berry to come.

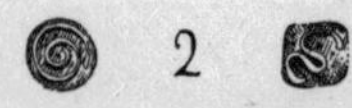

"It's not looking *so mint*," she said with a heavy sigh as she watched the rain fall. "What do you think, Hopper?" Dash asked. She put her hand out to the little creamy-white bunny she had found at her doorstep the day before. The little animal was wet and cold, so Dash had brought her inside. Once she had dried her off, she was fluffier than Dash had imagined, and Dash decided to call her Hopper. "You don't like the rain either," she said.

The little white bunny snuggled into Dash's hand.

"The rain had better stop if the Mint Jubilee is going to happen in the grove," Dash said.

Right now this was no place for a royal party.

In five days the Mint Jubilee was going to be in Candy Kingdom. When Princess Lolli and Prince Scoop, the ruling fairy princess and prince of Candy Kingdom, told her about the plans, Dash was superexcited. A mint celebration was always a good idea!

And Princess Lolli was happy to announce that her parents, Queen Sweetie and King Crunch, were coming from Sugar Kingdom for the grand party. The queen usually hosted the royal Mint Jubilee, so it was a big honor for Princess Lolli and Prince Scoop to have the party in Sugar Valley this year. Lolli planned to have a mint tea party for the royal family and the Candy Fairies in Peppermint Grove. Dash's job was to work on the mint candy wrapper designs with Pepper and Spera. But so far, those two fairies had not liked a single one of her drawings.

Dash was getting concerned about where the jubilee would be if the rain kept up. She wanted the party to be outside in Peppermint Grove with all the beautiful pink-and-white mints and green mint leaves. She held Hopper up to the window. "The rain had better stop soon," she said sadly.

Hopper twisted her little pink nose. Her long whiskers tickled Dash's fingers.

"At least we can keep dry inside," Dash told her. "But I miss my friends. You can meet Berry soon. You'll like her." Dash gave Hopper a piece of mint candy to nibble on and then read a book that Raina the Gummy Fairy had

given her, called *The Minty Clue.* Raina loved books. She even had her own library and looked after the treasured Fairy Code Book.

After a few chapters Dash looked out the window again. "You should know that Berry is always late, though," she told Hopper. "Chances are, she will be wearing a new outfit when she comes. She is the most stylish Candy Fairy."

Just then there was a knock at Dash's door.

Dash flew to the door, and her mouth fell open when she saw Berry. Berry was wearing a bright watermelon-colored poncho that covered her wings, and she was holding a huge orange-and-yellow umbrella.

"Holy peppermint!" Dash exclaimed.

"And I have the same outfit for you," Berry said, grinning. "But yours is red and white!"

Berry flew inside and handed Dash her package. "Try it on," Berry said. "We may not be able to enjoy a colorful Sun Dip, but we can definitely brighten Sugar Valley up with some colorful rain gear."

"This is *sugar-tastic*!" Dash cried. "You made all these?"

"Sure as sugar," Berry said. "I like working with fruit leather, which turns out to be excellent material for keeping off the rain." Berry removed her poncho and fluttered her wings. "And keeping wings dry," she added.

Dash slipped on her poncho and twirled her umbrella open. "This is *so mint*! Is everyone coming tonight?"

Berry nodded. "I just made deliveries to Gummy Forest, Chocolate Woods, and Caramel

Hills," she said. "Raina, Cocoa, and Melli are in for tonight. It is going to be a supersweet Sun Dip."

Hopper stuck her head out of Dash's dress pocket.

"Hello!" Berry said, looking down at the white fluffball. "Who are you?"

Dash laughed. "I took this little bunny in when the rain got bad last night," she explained. "I guess Candy Fairies aren't the only ones who don't like the rain. Minty bunnies don't either!"

"You can come too!" Berry said to the little white animal. "It will be a wet Sun Dip, but a happy one since we will be together. We're going to meet at the shed near Lollipop Landing."

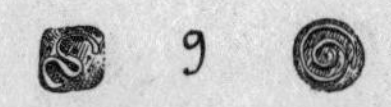

"Hopper and I will be there," Dash said.

Berry walked over to Dash's table. "Sweet strawberries! Are these your mint candy-wrapper designs? These are *sugar-tastic*," she said.

"Spera and Pepper won't think so," Dash mumbled.

"Oh, who cares what those bitter Mint Fairies think?" Berry said. "You did a great job. All that counts is whether Princess Lolli loves the designs. And she will. These are fantastic."

Dash wished she could be more like Berry and not care so much what other fairies thought, but Spera and Pepper had really not been nice when they met up the week before. The two older fairies made Dash feel uncomfortable when they were talking about her small size and making fun of her. Being small had nothing to do with having a good design for the candy wrappers! The two Mint Fairies were not as interested in helping as they were in gossiping and rolling their eyes at Dash. Dash was dreading seeing them again. She wished one of her true friends were working on the project with her.

"We may not even have the Mint Jubilee, anyway," Dash said. "Look at the mess in the grove. No one counted on the rain lasting for so long."

"After the rain comes a rainbow," Berry said. She gave her friend a tight squeeze. "Cheer up, Dash. I'll see you later."

Dash waved to Berry. Everything was so

soggy and wet. There were no rainbows in sight. Dash felt minty mad and bitter. And she definitely wasn't looking forward to meeting up with Spera and Pepper. If only she could race through the day and get to Sun Dip and see her friends!

Chapter 2

Supersweet Idea

Dash flew to a large white tent at the edge of Peppermint Grove. The new poncho Berry had made her worked very well, and Dash was able to fly faster than before. A few Mint Fairies were there already, working on plans for the Mint Jubilee. Dash spotted Spera and Pepper. They were giggling together. Dash

definitely didn't like being the third wheel.

Dash tried to think of her real friends and Sun Dip. In a few hours she would be sitting with them, huddled together under their new Berry-designed umbrellas and ponchos. The sweet thought helped Dash find the courage to take off her rain gear and fly over to the two bitter Mint Fairies.

"I made some new designs for the mint candy wrappers," Dash said. She showed Spera and Pepper some of her drawings.

The two mint fairies made sour faces and rolled their eyes.

"That looks a little babyish," Spera said.

"Not my taste," Pepper added.

Dash wasn't sure what to do. It wasn't as if these two fairies were in charge, but the three

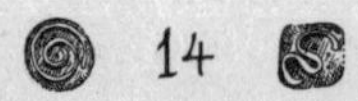

of them were supposed to work together. Though Dash wasn't sure that the other two had done any work at all!

"Look how small she is," Pepper whispered loudly to Spera. "How can she even fly with those tiny wings?"

Dash wanted to tell them that she was one of the fastest fliers in Sugar Valley and ask if they remembered that she had won many races. Instead, she lowered her wings and left her drawings on the table. She flew out of the tent and heard giggling as she left.

At Sun Dip, Dash tried not to think of Spera and Pepper. She was happy to see her friends in their colorful rain outfits, and she didn't want to spoil Sun Dip.

"Berry, you really are the best designer,"

Dash told her as she gazed at each of the rain outfits.

"I am stylish and dry!" Cocoa exclaimed.

"Me too!" Raina and Melli said at the same time.

Berry blushed. "I had to do something to get us all together. It had been too long." She turned to Dash. "How did it go today with Spera and Pepper?"

Dash wished that Berry hadn't said anything. Raina, Cocoa, and Melli were all giving her concerned looks.

Berry shrugged. "We all know that you are working with those two bitter mints," she said. "We're just trying to help."

"There is not much you can do," Dash said sadly. "They don't like my designs. I'm not sure what will happen if we don't agree." She twirled her new umbrella. "Maybe Princess Lolli will cancel the jubilee and none of this will matter."

Raina slid under Dash's umbrella to give her a hug. "Remember when we had those terrible rains and my gummies got all swirled? I was

so sad that the candies weren't perfect. And then the candies won a prize!" Raina smiled at Dash. "You have to stay positive and keep trying to make the mint wrappers and candies the best they can be. Those Mint Fairies will come around."

"And there is no way that Prince Scoop would let Princess Lolli cancel the party. He loves mint!" Melli added.

"We should just plan for rain," Cocoa said. "Even if the party is not in Peppermint Grove, we can have the festival in the castle or somewhere else."

Dash lowered her head. "But Peppermint Grove is the perfect place for the Mint Jubilee."

Berry thought for a moment and then exclaimed, "There should be rain hats for

everyone! Think about the fun, fashionable hats we could all wear."

"Only Berry would think of that," Melli said.

"Only Berry owns those kinds of hats!" Cocoa added.

Raina grinned. "Next up for Berry is making hats for all of us!"

Berry's wings were fluttering fast as she thought out loud. "Oh, I have tons of hats for you to choose from!" She clapped her hands. "Or I could even make some. Wouldn't that be *sugar-tastic*?"

"Yes," Raina agreed. "And you could make special hats for Princess Lolli and Queen Sweetie."

Berry clapped her hands. "That is one super-sweet idea," she said. "I am on the hat case!"

"But what about all the other details?" Dash said, pouting. "Like the location and the mint candy wrappers?"

"Dash, it will all get done," Cocoa told her. "Sure as sugar, this event will be the sweetest ever."

"More likely it will be the *wettest* ever," Dash told her.

"The royal tea party will go on," Melli declared. "Even in the rain!"

Dash knew her friends were trying to help, but they were missing the point. For her, the whole event was already ruined because of Spera and Pepper.

"Dash, you look so sad," Melli said. "You should talk to Princess Lolli. She would want to know how those fairies are treating you."

Dash shook her head. She didn't want to be known as the Candy Fairy who went to Princess Lolli for help with mean fairies. No, she would face these fairies on her own. "They would just say they didn't mean it or something like that," Dash replied. "And then they would be even more bitter because I'd gotten them in trouble."

"How about a chocolate caramel?" Cocoa asked her friends, trying to fix Dash's sour feelings. "Let's go sit on the benches in the shed."

"Thanks," Dash said.

The five fairies flew to the shed.

"Let's stop talking about the jubilee and start eating these Sun Dip treats," Dash said. She popped the chocolate caramel into her

mouth and motioned for her friends to do the same. “These are delicious!” she said. She held up the basket to her friends and quickly ended the discussion of the bitter Candy Fairies.

CHAPTER

3

Mint Meanies

The next morning Dash woke up to the sounds of raindrops hitting her window. She snuggled down in her fluffy pink-and-green cotton-candy blanket. The thought of going back to the party-planning tent was making Dash hide. She didn't want to see Pepper and Spera again.

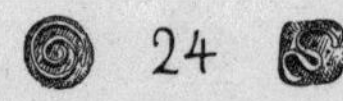

Dash tried to remember the positive talk from Sun Dip. Again she wished that her friends could be with her today. They all seemed to know what to say to the bitter, mean Mint Fairies.

Hopper hopped over to Dash and wiggled her whiskers.

"Oh, Hopper," Dash said. "Maybe you'll come with me?" The bunny hopped under a pillow. Dash laughed. "I feel the same way," she said. "If I didn't have to go, I would hide under the covers all day."

Dash grabbed her rain gear and her sketchpad. "Maybe my friends are right and today will be different," she said. She looked over at the large calendar hanging on the wall. There were three more days until the Mint Jubilee.

That was enough time to make and print the designs—and for the rain to stop. She knew that the five designs she had ready for today were good. This time the older fairies had to see that her work was minty perfect.

Feeling positive, Dash flew off to Peppermint Grove. She was very thankful for the large umbrella and poncho that Berry had made for her. She had missed speed flying!

At the tent set up in Peppermint Grove, many Mint Fairies were busy working on decorations. There were lots of details to attend to for a royal Mint Jubilee. There were fairies preparing mint tea, painting teacups, and making mint candies. Everything had to be peppermint perfect for the grand event.

Dash spotted Pepper and Spera. They were the only Mint Fairies not doing any work! They were sipping mint frappés and laughing loudly. Dash fluttered her wings a few times. Before she could even take her sketchpad from her bag, Pepper started laughing.

"What kind of poncho is that?" she asked.

"My friend Berry made it for me," Dash answered quickly. And then she got mad at herself for not coming up with a better reply.

"Very slick," Spera snickered.

"I have some more sketches for the mint candy wrappers," Dash said. She took off her poncho and hung it upon a hook. She wanted to move this conversation along. The less time she spent in the tent with the two mint meanies, the better.

"We have to show something to Princess Lolli this afternoon," Pepper told her.

"I heard she is coming here to see how the preparations for the jubilee are going," Spera added.

Dash knew that they were behind on the wrappers. The other Mint Fairies were waiting for them to complete the designs so that the new mint candies could be finished. She took her sketches and spread them out on the table.

But in a sour second Spera's mint frappé spilled. Dash tried to grab the drawings so they wouldn't get soaked, but some of the mint frappé got on the designs. "Careful," Dash scolded.

"Sorry," Spera said in an annoyed way. "You

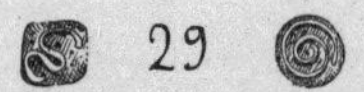

knocked the cup over when you took out your precious drawings."

Dash glared at Spera. She had never met such a bitter Mint Fairy.

"Even though you are small, you can make a big mess," Pepper said, giggling.

At that moment Dash didn't want to hear what they had to say about her drawings. She didn't wait to hear what the two of them would say about anything. She flew out of the tent.

The second she flew out Dash realized that she had forgotten to take her poncho!

"Ugh!" she cried as she sped over to a large weeping mint tree. Dash ducked under a tree and stood, trying to catch her breath. She was shivering and miserable. And quite sure that no one was watching.

But she was wrong.

Prince Scoop appeared by her side. “Hello, Dash,” he said very calmly.

Dash was so shocked to see the fairy prince that her mouth gaped open. She couldn’t speak or move! How was she going to explain herself?

“What brings you out here in the rain with no umbrella?” he asked.

Dash wiped her eyes quickly. She didn’t want him to see her crying. And she really didn’t want to tell the prince what was going on with the Mint Jubilee.

“Come with me,” Prince Scoop said. He pointed to a covered carriage with the royal unicorn Butterscotch standing ready. “This makes getting around in the rain a little safer,”

he said. "And faster," he added with a wink. He opened up his large ice-cream cone umbrella and escorted her to the dry carriage.

Dash had no choice but to follow. She sniffled a little and tried to stop her tears.

"Let's go have some tea at the castle," Prince Scoop told her. "I know there are some sweet treats in the throne room." He smiled at Dash, and she relaxed into the soft fruit-leather seat of the carriage. "Princess Lolli is off with her parents and making plans for the jubilee." He smiled again. "I guess you know all about that."

Dash nodded. A royal snack and some tea sounded very good to her. As the carriage flew up in the air behind Butterscotch, Dash looked back at the top of the mint tent at the

edge of Peppermint Grove. All her hard work and her designs were covered in mint frappé and likely being laughed at by Spera and Pepper. She sighed. At least she wasn't with the mint meanies anymore.

CHAPTER

4

Minty Sweet Treat

Butterscotch flew bravely through the heavy rain with a canopy above her. Dash was enjoying the ride in the covered carriage. She felt like a princess herself!

"Thank you for the ride," Dash said to Prince Scoop. "This was not what I thought I would be doing today!"

"I'm so happy you could come back to the castle with me," the prince told her. He smiled.

Dash's stomach rumbled. Prince Scoop was from Ice Cream Isles. No doubt his sweet treat would involve ice cream. And Dash loved ice cream! She was starting to feel better already. The farther she got from the mint meanies and Peppermint Grove, the better she felt. But then that thought made her sad. She was mad at herself for letting Spera and Pepper get to her.

Dash had just spotted Candy Castle when Prince Scoop asked, "You want to try taking the reins?"

Dash nodded. She had always wanted to try holding the reins of a royal unicorn pulling a fancy carriage. She reached out her hands.

"Gentle pulls," Prince Scoop told her. "You need to be firm but not harsh."

With Prince Scoop's coaching, Dash was able to steer the carriage.

"Great job," the prince said. "Let's try for a landing."

Dash saw the Royal Gardens below. "Are you sure?" she asked.

"You can do it. Stay focused," Prince Scoop said. "You want to keep your eyes on the horizon and guide her gently to the ground."

Dash did as the prince told her. This was much harder than steering a small sled!

"Nicely done!" Prince Scoop said as they landed. "You are a natural, Dash. You can take Butterscotch for a ride anytime."

Dash smiled. She loved being able to take the reins. "It was fun," she replied.

"Now come inside. I have a treat for you." He placed a large bucket of water in front of Butterscotch. "Thank you," he said to the unicorn.

"Yes, thank you," Dash said to Butterscotch. "You flew so quickly . . . even in the rain!"

Butterscotch nodded. Dash loved how fast unicorns could fly. There was nothing Dash loved more than a fast ride, either on her sled or in a carriage!

"I guess you haven't been racing much with all the rain," Prince Scoop said as they flew through the castle.

"No," Dash said sadly. "I really miss racing." She followed the prince into the throne room at the end of the long, wide hallway. The last time Dash had been in the throne room at Candy Castle, there was only one throne. That was before Princess Lolli was married. Now there were two thrones, for the royal princess and her prince.

"Let's sit here by the window," Prince Scoop said. He flew over to a cozy window seat at the far end of the room. "Those thrones aren't so comfortable," he said with a wink. "I prefer to sit here and look out at the gardens."

"The Royal Gardens are very pretty," Dash said. "My friends and I like to come here sometimes." Thinking of her friends, Dash got upset with herself for running out of the tent in Peppermint Grove. Berry or Cocoa would have stayed and stood up to Spera

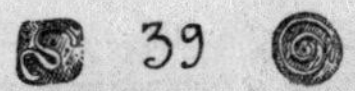

and Pepper. She should have done that.

"Dash, would you like a taste?" Prince Scoop asked. He was holding up a plateful of mint ice-cream sandwiches. He caught her eye and smiled. "I called your name a couple of times and you didn't answer. What is on your mind?"

Dash burst into tears. She didn't mean to start crying, but once she let herself she couldn't stop. Prince Scoop handed her a handkerchief.

"I want to tell you something," he said, leaning forward. "Not many Candy Fairies know this," he whispered.

Dash sniffled. "What?" she asked.

"When I was a young fairy, I was very small," he said. "I think I was smaller than you are now."

"No way," Dash said, blowing her nose.

Prince Scoop nodded. "It's true," he told her. "I was the smallest—and fastest—fairy in Ice Cream Isles. So I want you to know that I understand what you are going through now."

Dash looked up at the kind prince. *How much does he know?*

Prince Scoop reached into his pocket and handed Dash a small photograph. "This is me when I was young," he said. "You see? I was much smaller than you!"

She stared at the small fairy in the photograph. She could see how this fairy was Prince Scoop, but it was hard to think of him being that small! "That's really you?" Dash asked.

"Yes," he said with a chuckle. "Hard to believe,

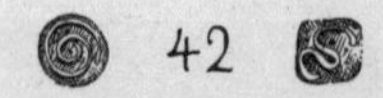

right? When I heard Spera and Pepper talking yesterday, I knew I had to show you this. I understand what it feels like to be smaller than everyone else. You can't let those fairies get you down."

Dash nodded. "You sound like my Candy Fairy friends," she said. "I know you're right, but it is hard. Those words hurt!"

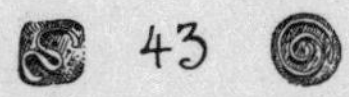

"Only if you let them," the prince said. "Fairies can be silly and jealous. You have so much talent, Dash. Don't let their words keep you from doing what you love."

"I hadn't thought of it that way," Dash said.

"I have something else for you," Prince Scoop said. He took a small box from his pocket and opened it. "I won this pin in a race when I was about your age," he said.

Dash held the small rainbow pin in her hand. "It's so beautiful," she said. She held up the candy-jeweled rainbow and admired the delicious colors.

"I thought you might want to make a necklace out of it," he told her. "This way you can remember that this rain will stop soon and a rainbow will come."

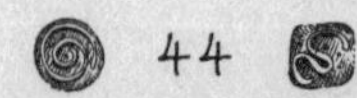

"This is the nicest gift that anyone has ever given me," Dash said. "I will cherish this forever. Thank you. Thank you for everything."

Prince Scoop bowed his head. "It is my pleasure," he said. "I hope you know that you can count on me. Now let's eat some ice cream, shall we?"

"How did you know that I love mint ice-cream sandwiches?" she asked. She loved how neatly the tiny ice-cream sandwiches were stacked on the plate.

"A little fairy princess might have let me in on that secret," he said. "And I happen to love these too! They come from Meringue Island. Some say they have healing power."

Dash smiled. "Oh, sure as sugar they do!" She took a bite and licked her lips. "These are even

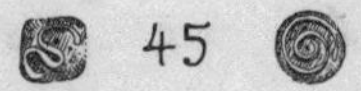

better than I remembered," she said.

Prince Scoop laughed. "These are good!" he exclaimed.

"This is *so mint*," Dash added. "Thank you, Prince Scoop. I'm feeling better." She squeezed the tiny rainbow in her hand. This was a minty sweet treat!

CHAPTER 5

Minty Day

Butterscotch took Dash home after her visit with Prince Scoop at Candy Castle. Dash couldn't believe the royal treatment she had gotten! She didn't arrive home until after Sun Dip, so she didn't have a chance to tell her friends about her trip to Candy Castle. She had sent a sugar fly note to Melli so she

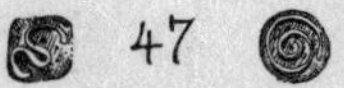

wouldn't worry, and asked her to tell the others. Dash would have a big report at Sun Dip tomorrow!

But first she had to face Spera and Pepper.

Dash got to sleep early and tried to think mint, sweet thoughts. She looped Prince Scoop's rainbow pin onto a chain and looked at herself in the mirror. The rainbow glittered and gave her an extra boost of confidence.

The next morning Dash was ready to get to work. She knew that one of her designs would be perfect for the jubilee. Even though it was still raining, Dash didn't let the rain soak her spirits.

"Today will be different, Hopper," Dash told the little white bunny.

Hopper snuggled into Dash's hand. Her white

fur was extra-soft. Dash fed her some treats and then reached up for a small basket. "Come with me to the work tent," Dash said. "I could use some friends around today."

Hopper hopped into the cozy basket. Dash put a cotton candy blanket on top of the small bunny. "Oh, you look so cute!" she exclaimed. She leaned in closer. "Thanks for coming along."

The first Mint Fairies that Dash saw as she flew over Peppermint Grove were Pepper and Spera. Touching her rainbow necklace, Dash knew she had to focus on her task and not on their mean words. She flew over to the table at the back of the tent and set up her work-station. The drawings that the mint frappé had spilled on were not there. Dash thought someone must have thrown those away.

She began to work on new designs. There was no one around to disturb her, and Dash spent the day drawing. Not once did she think about Spera and Pepper. They seemed to busy themselves at the frappé stand and didn't come by the tent at all. Dash was thankful for a chance to work in peace.

"Are these wrapper designs yours?" Menta asked, holding up Dash's designs from the day before as she flew over to Dash. Menta was a Mint Fairy who raced with Dash in sled races around Sugar Valley. Dash was happy to see a friendly face. The designs were a little wrinkled from the frappé, but there they were!

"Yes," she said. "Where did you get those? I thought they were ruined."

"I *knew* these were your designs," Menta replied.

"I thought it would be fun to use different mint colors like reds, greens, and pinks," Dash explained. "But I thought no one liked the designs. I've been working on some others."

"Other designs? Why would you do that?" Menta asked.

"Well, we need candy wrappers for the jubilee," Dash said.

Menta laughed. "Didn't anyone tell you?"

"Tell me what?" Dash asked.

"What are you fairies talking about?" Spera said as she flew over, with Pepper close behind.

Menta turned to see Pepper and Spera. "We're talking about the candy wrapper designs for the Mint Jubilee," she said. She held up one of Dash's drawings from the day before.

"Oh, we didn't do that," Spera said, wrinkling her nose.

"Really?" Menta asked. "Too bad, because Princess Lolli approved this design for the candy early this morning."

Spera and Pepper didn't say a word.

Dash grinned. "She did?" she asked. "Princess Lolli was here? She liked the drawing?"

Menta flapped her wings. "She was, and she loved your work, Dash. You don't need to do any more drawings. She approved this one."

"Did she know that I drew the design?" Dash said.

Menta rolled her eyes. "Well, everyone knew Spera and Pepper had nothing to do with it."

"Hey!" Spera cried. "That's not fair."

"But it's true," Menta said, winking at Dash. "Good work, Dash," she said.

Dash couldn't believe her ears. Princess Lolli loved her design!

"Good morning!" Prince Scoop cried as he swooped into the tent. "I just heard the sweet news," he said to Dash.

"Thanks," Dash said.

"Now you have to come outside," Prince Scoop told her. "The rain has stopped!"

Dash followed Prince Scoop out of the tent. High in the sky was a faint rainbow reaching across the sky. She could just make out the seven bands of color reaching across the horizon.

"A rainbow!" Dash replied.

"Yes, a rainbow," the prince said. "You see,

the rain did stop. And Lolli loved your design."

"But everything is still a soggy, minty mess," Dash said, looking around the grove. Puddles of water were everywhere, and heavy branches lay on the ground.

The prince looked around. "Yes, I suppose that is true," he said. "But for now the rain has stopped. We can all fly freely. That is surely something to celebrate."

Dash had to agree. After all, her design was approved and there would be no rain for Sun Dip!

"I'm going to get home and get ready for Sun Dip," Dash said. "I can't wait to see my friends tonight. I have so much to tell them!" She watched Prince Scoop smile. "Would you like to come?" she asked the prince in a quiet voice. She was a little embarrassed to ask, but she hoped he would say yes.

"I would love to come!" Prince Scoop replied. "You know Lolli will be busy with making plans for the jubilee, but I am free. Thank you very much for the kind invitation."

"Everyone will be so happy to see you," Dash said. "This will be an extra-sweet Sun Dip."

Dash flew home without holding an umbrella. She loved how the cool air felt on her wings. This was the sweetest day!

Sun Dip Sweetness

When Dash arrived home, she felt so happy. She had not stopped smiling since she had heard the news about Princess Lolli's liking her design. And for the first time in weeks she and her friends would be able to sit along the shores of Red Licorice Lake and watch Sun Dip without umbrellas!

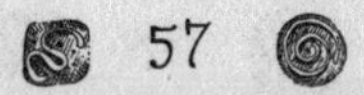

"Come, Hopper," Dash said. "We've got lots to do before we meet up at Red Licorice Lake. I want to be sure to have some minty good snacks for everyone."

Dash got busy making Sun Dip treats. She wanted to make these sweet treats extra-special and minty! After her mint swirl chocolates were done, she peeked out her window. A sugar fly landed on her shoulder. The little fly had a note from Raina!

"'We are all meeting for Sun Dip tonight. You'd better be there! We miss you,'" Dash read. She turned to Hopper. "I can't wait!"

Looking up at the sky, Dash could see the sun just above the peaks of the Frosted Mountains. She gathered up her treats in her basket and set out for Red Licorice Lake.

Raina, Cocoa, and Melli were spreading out their blankets when Dash arrived. Berry came right after Dash. It seemed all her friends were excited to gather for this Sun Dip.

"Dash, Princess Lolli loved your design!" Berry said before her feet even touched the ground.

"Hot chocolate!" Cocoa cried. "That is the sweetest news!"

"And I didn't get a chance to share it!" Dash said, with her hands on her hips.

"Sorry!" Berry said. "I just heard and I was so happy for you!"

"You see?" Raina said, grinning. "I knew those bitter Mint Fairies didn't know what they were talking about. Princess Lolli loved the design? Tell us everything!"

Dash filled her friends in on Menta's report and told them all about her visit with Prince Scoop. She showed them the rainbow pin on the chain around her neck.

"That is the sweetest thing," Raina cooed.

"Prince Scoop is the best," Melli added.

Berry took her sketchbook from her bag. "I want you to see these outfits I drew," she said. "This might be a wet Mint Jubilee, but it is going to be the most talked-about fashion event in Sugar Valley if I have anything to say about it!"

Raina laughed. "One hundred percent!" she exclaimed. Raina looked through Berry's sketchbook. "These designs are amazing, Berry. We are all going to look so *sugar-tastic*!"

"I love the hats," Melli added. She pointed to one on the page. "Can you really make these by tomorrow?"

"Sure as sugar," Berry said proudly. "It will be a close finish, but I am sure I can deliver."

Melli put out her caramels on a plate for her friends. "Even though the *Daily Scoop* reports that the day is not going to be all rainbows and clear skies, this will be a Mint Jubliee to remember," she said.

Dash flew up in the air. Her wings were moving so fast that she took flight. "I just had the most brilliant, delicious idea!" she exclaimed. Berry laughed. "Slow down, Dash," she said. "Come back down and tell us."

"This is not a race," Raina said, giggling. "Though it is beginning to feel like one. The royal Mint Jubilee is in two days!"

Dash came back down to the blanket. "If we are going to make this event the best, we're going to have to work super fast."

"I'm up for that," Cocoa said. "What are you thinking, Dash?"

"We can make our own blue skies and rainbows!" Dash exclaimed. "We can decorate the

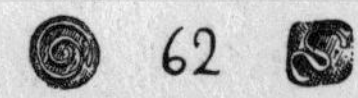

ballroom at Candy Castle with rainbows and make the room minty colorful!"

"That is the most delicious idea ever!" Berry cried. "We could definitely come up with some colorful decorations. Very smart, Dash!"

"Sugar-tastic!" Raina cried. "But can we keep the hats, too? I was getting excited about a Berry original design." She smiled at Berry.

"Sweet strawberries, of course!" Berry exclaimed.

"That is a supersweet idea," Melli said.

Cocoa put up her hand. "Hold on," she said. "We need permission from the castle to change the place and theme of the jubilee."

"What's this about the jubilee changing?" Prince Scoop asked as he landed next to Dash.

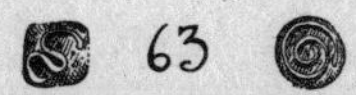

Berry, Raina, Melli, and Cocoa were shocked to see Prince Scoop standing on Dash's blanket.

"Um, I forgot to mention that we were going to have a special guest for Sun Dip tonight," Dash said, blushing. In all the excitement, she had forgotten to mention that she had invited Prince Scoop. "I guess this was a good time for you to come!" she said to the prince.

Berry pulled her cotton-candy woven wrap around her. "Oh, Prince Scoop," she said, "Dash didn't tell us you'd be joining us. We're really not prepared for such a special visitor."

"I wish we had known so we could have prepared a big feast," Melli said, looking

down at just the few bites of sweet treats left.

"Oh, Berry," Dash said, "you look perfect! And Prince Scoop doesn't care about all that formal stuff."

"Please sit on my blanket," Melli said, flying over to sit with Cocoa to make room for the prince.

"It's *so mint* that Prince Scoop came, don't you think?" Dash said, grinning. "Make him feel comfortable!"

Prince Scoop laughed. "Oh, please," he said. He settled down on Melli's blanket. "I am happy to be here. I'm glad you weren't expecting me. I wanted to come see you without being all royal." He winked at Dash. "This is really nice. Especially with the rain stopping."

"But it's still so soggy," Melli said. "Do you think the jubilee will be moved?"

"I don't know," Prince Scoop replied. "But it seems you were thinking of some plan. I bet Princess Lolli would love to hear it."

"Well then, we'll have to go see her first thing in the morning," Dash said. She held out her mint treat to Prince Scoop. She was so glad that he was there to share this Sun Dip with her friends. Dash was sure this would turn out to be the best royal Mint Jubilee.

Chapter 7

Mint Rainbow

Dash met up with her four Candy Fairy friends early the next morning. Everyone was feeling happy—and dry! The rain had stopped, and the plan was to fly to Candy Castle together for their meeting with Princess Lolli and Prince Scoop. Dash was very nervous about asking Princess Lolli to

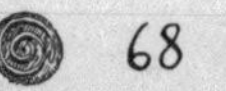

change the location of the royal Mint Jubilee.

"Are you ready?" Raina asked.

"Yes," Dash said. "I'm so glad everyone is coming with me. Cocoa even said she drew up some pictures so Princess Lolli could see what we're talking about."

"Where is Cocoa?" Berry asked. "You mean Cocoa is the last to arrive? I don't believe it!"

Melli laughed. "For once Berry is not the last one," she said.

"I'm here!" Cocoa shouted from above. "I just wanted to finish up some drawings."

"Let's go," Dash said. "I want to get to the castle already. I am going to burst if I don't talk to Princess Lolli about the jubilee soon."

"We don't want that to happen," Berry said.

The five friends flew to Candy Castle, but

Dash quickly took the lead . . . and then flew with superspeed. Dash was the first of her friends to land in the Royal Gardens. Even when she landed, Dash's wings didn't stop moving.

What if Princess Lolli doesn't like the rainbow idea? she thought. *What if the princess doesn't want to have the jubilee at Candy Castle?*

The bitter thoughts were circling in Dash's head, and she flew in circles around the garden to cool off.

"Hey, Dash," Cocoa called, "this wasn't supposed to be a race! You were flying so fast! And you are still moving!" She landed in the garden, trying to catch her breath. "Please come down and rest for a minute. I could barely keep up." She squinted at the

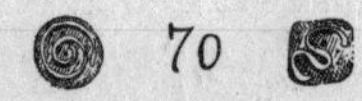

sky. "I don't even see Melli, Raina, and Berry!"

"When I am nervous, I fly faster," Dash said. She landed next to Cocoa and shrugged. "Sorry!"

"Dash, don't look so worried," Cocoa said. "I am sure Princess Lolli is going to love your ideas."

"I hope so," Dash said. "I want to make sure everything is perfect for the meeting."

"Do you want to see decoration sketches?" Cocoa told her. She reached into her bag and took out her sketchbook. "It's just like we talked about at Sun Dip."

Dash smiled. "Thanks, Cocoa," she said. Dash flipped through the pages. Cocoa was such a good artist. "I knew I could count on you. These sketches look *so mint*!"

Melli, Raina, and Berry finally flew over the Royal Gardens. All of them were breathing heavily—and looking exhausted!

"You made it," Cocoa said.

"Dash was flying superfast," Raina said. She wiped her forehead. "How did you keep up?"

Cocoa smiled. "Chocolate rush, I guess," she said. "I was excited to share these drawings with Dash." She patted her sketchbook. "I love the rainbow idea, and I know Princess Lolli will too."

"Sure as sugar!" Melli exclaimed.

"And the castle ballroom is the perfect place for the party," Raina added. "It's *sugar-tastic*!"

Berry squeezed Dash's hand. "Don't worry," she said. "I know Princess Lolli is going to be so happy about this plan."

Melli laughed. "I'm not even worried!" she exclaimed. "And you know I worry about *everything.*"

"Let's head inside," Berry said, moving toward the front gate of the castle. "Princess Lolli and Prince Scoop are expecting us."

The five friends flew over to the royal guards. The guards announced their arrival to the princess and prince, and the Candy Fairies found the royal couple in the throne room.

"Welcome," Princess Lolli said. "This is such a treat to see you all."

Dash smiled at Prince Scoop. She understood that he had not shared their thoughts about the Mint Jubilee with Princess Lolli. After all, it was Dash's idea, and she should be the one to ask Princess Lolli.

Cocoa held out her sketchbook as Dash spoke about the rainbow decorations. It was easy to see how excited Princess Lolli was about the theme and decorations.

"Do you think everyone will be comfortable here in the ballroom?" Princess Lolli asked Prince Scoop. "We have never had a jubilee inside the castle before."

"Why not?" Prince Scoop asked. "I think we'd be able to make it work." He looked up at Cocoa and Dash. "These designs are really delicious. Your drawings are terrific."

Princess Lolli took Dash's hand. "Thank you for taking the lead on this," she said. "You have done a *sweet-tacular* job."

"And now we have a ton of work to do to make this all happen," Dash said with a big grin.

"Very well," Princess Lolli said. "We can't wait to see you later."

Prince Scoop flew over to Dash. "I'm so proud of you and your friends. This is going to be *so mint*!" He winked and flew after Princess Lolli. "See you later," he called.

Dash led her friends back to Peppermint Grove, where she told the other Mint Fairies about the change of location.

"Sweet mint!" Menta exclaimed. "We'll get right on bringing all the decorations and candy to the castle. Good job, Dash."

Dash felt proud and smiled at her friends. And then she saw Spera and Pepper.

"Good idea," Spera said.

"Everyone seems to like the change," Pepper added.

Dash couldn't tell if they were being nice or not. But to her it didn't matter. She was feeling so happy.

"Are you two going to help, or what?" Menta asked. She patted Dash on the back and moved Spera and Pepper along to a dipping station.

Dash was grateful to Menta for distracting the mint meanies. She put her hand on Prince Scoop's rainbow charm. She felt it must have magical powers. Everything seemed to be going perfectly now. Thinking about rainbows and all the decorations for the jubilee made Dash smile. Things didn't seem to be a minty mess anymore. In fact, today was a supercool mint rainbow!

CHAPTER

8

A Royal Assignment

Early the next morning Dash flew to Candy Castle. She was surprised at how many other Candy Fairies were already there when she arrived. Everyone was working hard to change the royal ballroom into a *mint-tacular* setting.

The room was bright with red, white, green, and pink colors, and there were tiny rainbows

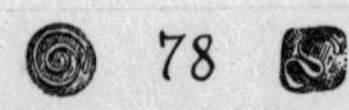

scattered around the room. The decorations looked so sweet, and Dash was proud of the Mint Fairies and other Candy Fairies who had pitched in to help. Today was the royal Mint Jubilee!

Across the room, Dash spotted Cocoa and Melli sitting on the floor. They were surrounded by seven cans of rainbow-colored sugar paint.

"You are here early," Dash said, flying over to them. She looked down at what they were painting. "And those tiny rainbows are *so mint*!"

"Thanks," Cocoa said. She leaned back to admire their work. "We're almost done with these."

"These rainbows are going to be part of the

centerpieces," Melli told Dash. She pointed to the opposite corner. "You have to check out Menta's wall hanging. She is an amazing artist."

Dash smiled. "And so are you," she said. She saw how carefully her friends had painted the mini sugar rainbows. They would look so delicious in the center of each table. "I can't believe how fast this room has changed. This is going to be the sweetest Mint Jubilee that Sugar Valley has ever seen!"

"I just wish my parents would be able to see it," Princess Lolli said, coming up behind Dash.

"Wait, what?" Dash said. She looked at Princess Lolli's face and saw that the princess had been crying. This was not like her to be so sad. "What do you mean?"

"The rain has made traveling very difficult," Princess Lolli said. "This morning there were more reports of rain on the way, and I don't think it is safe for them to fly here."

"Oh, bittersweet," Cocoa whispered.

"But they have to come!" Dash blurted out. "This is the first time the Mint Jubilee will be in Candy Kingdom! And Berry made special hats for you and the queen!"

Melli stood up and put her arm around Dash. "Dash," she scolded, "don't make Princess Lolli feel worse. I'm sure she is trying to think of a way to get them here."

Princess Lolli shook her head. "My parents don't have a covered carriage," she said. "And with all that is going on here, Scoop and I can't fly out to get them."

She turned away and flew out of the ball-room.

"Hot caramel," Melli said. "I have never seen Princess Lolli so upset."

Cocoa shook her head. "This would be the first Mint Jubilee that the queen and king have missed."

Dash's wings fluttered. "Well, we can't have that!" she said.

"Where are you going?" Cocoa called. "Dash!"

Dash followed Princess Lolli out of the room and found her by a window in the grand hall. She was sitting on the window seat, looking up at the dark, gray sky.

"I have an idea," Dash said. "I can fly up to Sugar Castle in the covered carriage and get your parents." She stood tall and brave.

"Are you sure?" Princess Lolli said. She turned to give Dash a long, serious look. "You feel comfortable enough to steer the carriage?"

"I know that I can handle Butterscotch and get there safely," Dash went on. "Ask Prince Scoop—he let me drive the carriage before. I flew in the covered carriage with Prince Scoop the other day, and it was very dry and safe."

"He let you drive?" Princess Lolli asked, looking surprised.

Suddenly Dash felt horrible. She didn't want to get the prince in trouble. "I begged him," Dash went on. "It wasn't his fault. I was feeling so sad about, well . . . things being so minty and the rain and everything." Dash sighed. "But I was really good at driving the carriage, and Butterscotch listened to me."

Princess Lolli started to laugh. "Oh, Dash, I'm not mad!" she exclaimed. "I'm relieved! Here I was, thinking that Scoop and I couldn't go get my parents with all the work to be done here, and now you can do this for us!"

Dash bowed her head. "It would be my honor to go and get Queen Sweetie and King Crunch," she said.

"You would fly the royal carriage with Butterscotch all the way to Sugar Kingdom?" Princess Lolli asked. "It is a lot to ask of you. Are you sure?"

Dash stood up a little straighter. "I'd be honored," she said. Then she looked back at all the Candy Fairies in the ballroom. "But I am not the bravest or biggest fairy," she said quietly. "Are you sure you'd want me to go?"

"You have the biggest heart," Prince Scoop said. He came up and gave Dash a tight squeeze. "And we believe in you. Plus, I've seen you drive!" He looked at Princess Lolli. "Dash is a real natural. In fact, I should have thought of it myself."

Princess Lolli hugged Dash. "I am sure you can handle the royal carriage and Butterscotch," she said. "Thank you for doing this."

"Can I bring my friends too?" Dash asked. She thought of Melli and Cocoa inside the ballroom. The journey would be much more fun with them. And she knew Raina and Berry would not want to miss out on the adventure.

"Of course," Princess Lolli replied. "My parents

would love that!" she said, smiling. "And you will have fun together."

"Thank you!" Dash said.

"You should leave soon," Prince Scoop told Dash. "Go tell the others and meet back here before midday. There is another storm coming our way."

Princess Lolli smiled. "Today just got a whole lot brighter," she said, "even if there is more rain due to roll in. It will not dampen our royal Mint Jubilee party one bit!"

Dash grinned. "Sure as sugar," she said. "You can count on me and my friends." She flew off to tell her friends of the royal assignment they were about to take.

CHAPTER

9

Sweet Welcomes

The five friends quickly flew to the Royal Stables together to get the carriage and Butterscotch ready for the journey to Sugar Kingdom.

"Are you *sure* you can handle this?" Melli asked. Her eyes were wide as she took in the size of the carriage. "Why couldn't one of the guards go?" she asked.

"Because not all the guards know how to ride Butterscotch when she is pulling this carriage," Dash told her. "Besides, we're helping Princess Lolli and Prince Scoop. It's going to be great. You'll see."

"Oh no," Melli cried, looking at the sky. "The rain has started again."

"That's all right," Dash told her. "This is why we're taking the covered carriage. It will be fine."

"This is the biggest carriage I have ever seen!" Cocoa exclaimed.

"Check out these seats," Berry said, flopping onto the cushioned bench. "This is definitely a royal ride."

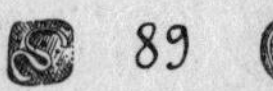

"We could fit ten more Candy Fairies in here," Raina said as she looked around.

Dash knew her friends were a little nervous about the trip, but she wasn't. She had confidence that she could handle the ride. It felt good taking this task on. For the past week she had been feeling so low. This was going to be one minty cool ride!

The rain was coming down hard, so Dash and her friends helped get Butterscotch prepared. Carefully, they put a large red rain shield around the unicorn. It was a giant canopy that covered her wings and protected them from the rain. Butterscotch looked ready to ride through any storm.

Dash took away Butterscotch's feed bucket.

She gave the sweet unicorn a kiss on the nose. “We’re going to be a great team again,” she said. Then she called out to her friends, “Everyone in! We’re ready to ride.”

The Candy Fairies climbed inside the carriage just as Princess Lolli and Prince Scoop flew inside the stable.

"We're here to see you off, " Princess Lolli said.

"Sure as sugar," Dash replied, grinning. "We put up the canopy and we're ready to go."

Prince Scoop smiled. "I know you'll be careful," he said. "Butterscotch knows the way. Remember, a slight tug on the reins. And don't go too fast."

"I remember," Dash said. "Don't worry." She looked over her shoulder at her friends. "I know, it's not a race."

"That's for sure," Melli said, settling into her seat.

"Thank you again for going to Sugar Kingdom

today," Princess Lolli said. "We'll see you back here soon."

Dash sat up on the bench and took the reins. "A steady hand," she said, thinking of her ride with Prince Scoop. Butterscotch trotted forward and Prince Scoop opened up the stable door wider.

"Safe travels," the prince called.

"See you soon," Dash replied. She took hold of the reins, and Butterscotch leaped up in the air.

The rain made a soft drumming sound on the carriage roof, and Dash leaned back in the seat. "Everyone okay?" she called.

"We're fine," Raina answered.

"This really is the way to travel!" Berry said, stretching out on the seat.

"And we can stay dry!" Melli added. "Even Butterscotch is staying dry."

"Choc-o-rific!" Cocoa exclaimed.

Prince Scoop was right about Butterscotch's knowing the way. Even with raindrops falling,

the unicorn knew the route. Dash kept her eyes open for anything that might cause any alarm or problems, but the journey went very smoothly.

"I see the palace!" Raina called.

Down to the left, Dash saw the top of the palace as well—the bright white sugar turrets of the old palace.

"So mint!" Dash exclaimed. "Hold on, we're coming in for a landing!"

Dash held the reins and guided Butterscotch down to the palace garden, just as Prince Scoop had shown her when they had landed at Candy Castle. She took a deep breath as she felt the unicorn's hooves touch the ground.

In a flash the royal guards of the palace

came out to the carriage. A red fruit leather carpet was rolled up to the carriage door, and a rainbow of colorful umbrellas appeared.

"Why, this is a sweet welcome," Dash said.

A large caramel trumpet sounded, and the king and queen walked out of the palace and down the red carpet. The door to the carriage was opened and the royal couple peered inside.

"So nice to see you all!" King Crunch said. "Thank you for coming to get us."

"We never did get a covered carriage," Queen Sweetie told the Candy Fairies. "Lolli has been after us to do that, but lucky for us you were able to come!"

"It is our pleasure," Dash said. "Please have a seat and we'll be on our way."

Dash was bursting with pride. She knew she

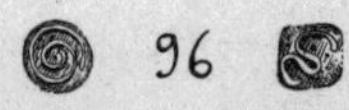

was likely speaking way too fast, but she was so excited to be driving the king and queen back to Candy Castle.

The royal couple sat down and gave gifts of sugar stars to each of the Candy Fairies. Dash wanted to join in on their conversation, but she kept her focus on the sky ahead.

"We've got this," Dash said to Butterscotch. "We're almost there."

The ride back to Candy Castle felt much shorter to Dash. Maybe she really was getting the hang of driving the carriage. The tricky part was landing. She took the approach slowly and held the reins tightly.

"Easy, Butterscotch," Dash called.

Butterscotch responded to Dash's command, and the landing was as smooth as a licorice stick. Everyone in the carriage cheered and applauded Dash.

"Dash, come here so we can give Queen Sweetie her gift," Berry said.

Queen Sweetie looked surprised. "What do you mean?"

"Because of all the rain," Dash said, "we came up with a different theme for the jubilee this year."

Berry handed the queen a hatbox. "We're all wearing colorful hats to tea," she said.

"Sometimes you have to make your own rainbows," Dash said, smiling.

"I couldn't agree with you more," Queen Sweetie said. She opened the box and squealed with delight. "How scrumptious!"

"Let's get this party started," King Crunch said, and opened the door.

Dash was so happy as they all piled out of the carriage and headed into the castle to begin the festive Mint Jubilee.

CHAPTER 10

Mint Truth

When Dash walked into the Candy Castle ballroom, her mouth hung open. "Holy peppermint," she said, looking around. "The Candy Fairies were certainly busy while we were away. This place looks like a minty wonderland."

In the time that it had taken to fly to Sugar

Kingdom and back, all the decorations had been put up and the rainbow centerpieces had been perfectly placed on all the tables. The ballroom had been completely changed into a minty wonderland full of white, red, pink, and green colors and candies. Dash felt so proud of the work all the Candy Fairies had done to make this event happen.

"It looks delicious," King Crunch declared. He flew over to Princess Lolli and Prince Scoop. "It's like the jubilee was meant to be here all along. No rain can dampen the spirits of these Candy Fairies!"

"Dash, you have done a great service to everyone," Queen Sweetie said. She leaned in closer to her. "Lolli filled me in on your ideas for this event. You are a minty marvel!"

Dash blushed. “Thanks, Queen Sweetie.”

“Moving the event inside to the castle was minty brilliant,” the queen went on. “You really saved the day.”

When Dash turned around, she saw Spera and Pepper standing nearby. She couldn’t help but feel good even though she knew they’d be talking about her. After all, they were not getting compliments from the queen. And they still had sour expressions on their faces!

She wondered what they were thinking. They had been so mean and negative about everything. At that moment Dash decided that she really didn’t need to think about what Spera and Pepper thought! What mattered most was what she felt. And right now she was feeling extra minty good!

On one of the tables there were large trays of mints in the beautiful wrappers that Dash had designed. Dash took a few and put them in her bag. For sure Hopper would want to have some of those treats. She would tell the bunny lots of sweet stories tonight!

"Dash, come put your hat on," Berry called. She waved Dash over to where her friends were gathered. Melli, Cocoa, Raina, and Berry all had put on their new colorful hats and were holding teacups. They looked so sweet. Dash was the luckiest Candy Fairy to have such loyal, true friends.

Before Dash reached her friends,

Prince Scoop took her aside. "Your command of the carriage was outstanding," he told Dash. He handed her a cup of mint tea. "I was really proud of how you flew forward to help out. Plus, you had a perfect landing."

"You are a very good teacher," Dash replied, smiling. "Thank you for taking the time to teach me. And for . . . well, everything," she said, trying not to gush. She touched the rainbow charm on her necklace. "Our talk helped so much, and so has this pin. You are the best fairy prince a Candy Fairy could ask for."

Prince Scoop laughed and gave Dash a hug. "I'm glad," he said. "I'm just so happy this day worked out. And everyone

got such nice-looking hats!" He fixed a green fedora on his head. "What do you think? Even I got a fancy new hat for the occasion!"

"Dash has a new hat too!" Berry said as she flew over. She was holding a beautiful pink-and-green hat made of twisted mint leaves and candy.

"Thanks, Berry," Dash said. She put her stylish hat on and smiled. "You all look so mint!" she told her friends as they flew around her. "Thank you again for coming with me to Sugar Kingdom."

The royal Mint Jubilee was a great, sweet success. At the end of the evening Princess Lolli gave Dash a hug. "Dash, everyone is talking about your mint candy designs," she said. "You should be very proud."

Dash grinned. She was one hundred percent mint happy. "Thank you," she said.

"Your positive attitude rubbed off on everyone!" Prince Scoop said. "Look around! I have never seen a Mint Jubilee so well attended."

"Or so fashionable!" Berry exclaimed, touching her hat. "Doesn't everyone look so *sugar-tastic* in their hats and drinking mint tea?"

Dash nodded as her friends circled around her. "I'm never going to just wait for the rainbow. I'm always going to make my own!" she declared.

Her friends gave a little cheer. Dash felt a

minty rush of joy. No matter what happened with those mint meanies, she knew who her real friends were and who she could count on. As far as Dash could tell, everyone was having a great time. Except for Spera and Pepper—they never smiled once!

"Look at Spera and Pepper." Dash pointed across the room. The two Mint Fairies were standing together, looking bitter. "They didn't want to wear hats, and now they are the only ones not wearing them."

"It must get stale and old being so minty mad all the time," Cocoa said.

"I think they're used to it," Dash said, giggling. For the first time she really didn't care. "Come on, let's get some more mint treats!"

The royal Mint Jubilee may have been

different from what everyone expected, but it was sure sweeter than Dash had ever imagined. Dash and her friends had made their own rainbows and turned the event into something *sugar-tastic*! And that was the real mint truth.

Mermaid Tales
Exciting under-the-sea adventures with
Shelly and her mermaid friends!
Trouble at Trident Academy
Battle of the Best Friends
A Whale of a Tale
Danger in the Deep Blue Sea
The Lost Princess
The Secret Sea Horse
A Royal Tea
The Polar Bear Express
MermaidTalesBooks.com
FROM ALADDIN • SIMONANDSCHUSTER.COM/KIDS • EBOOK EDITIONS ALSO AVAILABLE

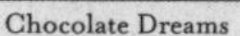 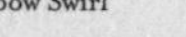

Chocolate Dreams | Rainbow Swirl | Caramel Moon | Cool Mint | Magic Hearts

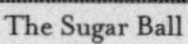

Gooey Goblins | The Sugar Ball | A Valentine's Surprise | Bubble Gum Rescue | Double Dip | Jelly Bean Jumble

The Chocolate Rose | A Royal Wedding | Marshmallow Mystery | Frozen Treats | The Sugar Cup | Sweet Secrets

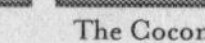 

Taffy Trouble | The Coconut Clue | Rock Candy Treasure | A Minty Mess

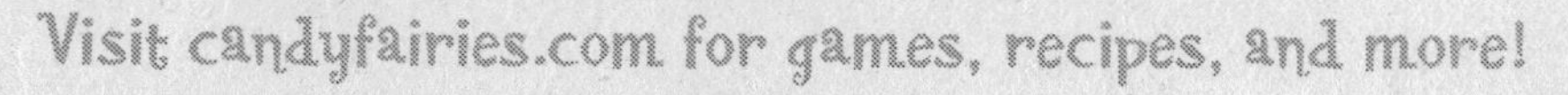

EBOOK EDITIONS ALSO AVAILABLE

FROM ALADDIN • SIMONANDSCHUSTER.COM/KIDS

Join Willa and the Chincoteague ponies on their island adventures!
Misty Inn
Welcome Home!
KRISTIN EARHART
Misty Inn
Buttercup Mystery
Misty Inn
Runaway Pony
KRISTIN EARHART
Misty Inn
Finding Luck
KRISTIN EARHART
EBOOK EDITIONS ALSO AVAILABLE
ALADDIN
simonandschuster.com/kids